In an instant they were off—
the hare soon out of sight,
the tortoise plodding step by patient step.

Aesop's Fables

JERRY PINKNEY

AESOP'S FABLES

chronicle books · san francisco

Typeset in 17.5 point Bodoni Twelve ITC Book.
The illustrations in this book were rendered in pencil, colored pencil, and watercolors.
Manufactured in China, July 2009.

Library of Congress Cataloging-in-Publication Data
Aesop's Fables. English. Selections. 2000.
Aesop's Fables / Jerry Pinkney
p. cm.
Summary: A collection of nearly sixty fables from Aesop, including such familiar ones as "The Grasshopper and the Ants," "The North Wind and the Sun," "Androcles and the Lion," "The Troublesome Dog," and "The Fox and the Stork."
ISBN 978-1-58717-000-3
1. Fables, Greek–Translations into English. [1. Fables. 2. Folklore.]
I. Aesop. II. Pinkney. III. Title
PZ8.2.A254 2000 398.24′52–dc21 00-24194

10 9 8

This product conforms to CPSIA 2008.

Chronicle Books LLC
680 Second Street, San Francisco, California 94107

www.chroniclekids.com

To Shelly Fogelman–

Thank you for helping me to see a bigger picture.

J. P.

❖

CONTENTS

INTRODUCTION

The fables of Aesop have always conjured up for me an astounding range of unforgettable images, from the poignant to the delightfully absurd: a humble Greek slave and his steadfast lion friend who would one day save the man from a tragic fate; a crafty wolf lurking under a loose sheep's skin; a carefree, fiddling grasshopper who puts off for tomorrow what he should do today. From my earliest years my parents used the powerful themes from the tales to teach my siblings and me about human folly and virtue. At the time, though, I was only interested in the stories' compelling characters and their fast-paced, colorful narratives; I never really wondered about their purpose or origins.

In fact, the real Aesop was born a slave about the year 620 B.C. in the ancient republic of Greece, where he was later granted freedom as a reward for his learning and wit. Though he died about 565 B.C., for years his clever wisdom was passed down orally from generation to generation. Somewhere around 300 B.C., about 200 stories were gathered into a collection called *Assemblies of Aesopic Tales*. No one knows how many of the narratives attributed to Aesop were actually composed by him. Interestingly, motifs from many of them occur in the storytelling traditions of a variety of cultures–proof of the universality of the themes and lessons of these tales.

In time my own awareness of the deep truths of the fables' morals has grown; I see now how what was simply entertainment to me as a child has become an essential part of my life. It's surprising how often I find myself recalling a moral without its corresponding story, and vice versa. Each stands effectively and wholly on its own, yet together their impact is even greater. This project has enabled me to wed the fondly remembered narratives of my youth with an appreciation of their ongoing lessons in my adult life. I hope this sampling of what I consider to be some of the best well-known and lesser-known fables will speak to all ages of readers, through all ages, as they have for me.

–Jerry Pinkney

THE SHEPHERD BOY AND THE WOLF

Every day a poor shepherd sent his son to take their few sheep out to pasture. "We can't afford to lose even one," he would tell the boy, "so keep a close eye on them. And if you see a wolf, shout as loudly as you can, and the whole village will come to drive the wolf away."

Day after day the shepherd's boy sat alone in the meadow. "I wish a wolf would come!" he said to himself one day. "At least then something would happen."

Then the boy had an idea. Jumping to his feet, he cried, "Wolf! Wolf!" as loudly as he could. Sure enough, the shepherd and the farmer, the milkmaid and the baker, all came running. But when they reached the meadow, all they found was the shepherd's boy, laughing at their trouble. "There's no wolf here!" he shouted.

"We've better things to do than run all this way for nothing," muttered the angry townsfolk to one another.

That night the shepherd's boy promised his father he would never play such a trick again. But a few days later, as he was watching the sheep, the boy became restless again. Thinking of how amusing his last trick had been, he drew in his breath and shouted, "Wolf! Wolf!"

Again all the villagers came running. But when they saw no wolf, they again grew angry. "There was a wolf, I swear!" the shepherd's boy insisted. "He ran away when he heard you coming!"

But no one believed him, and they went home grumbling.

The very next day the shepherd's boy took the sheep to the meadow again. But just as the sheep started to graze, he saw a dark shape with glowing eyes lurking in the shadow of the trees. "Wolf!" he shouted as loudly as he could. The animal growled and crept closer. "Wolf! Wolf!" cried the frightened boy, but no one came. And the wolf leaped on one of the sheep, dragging it away into the forest.

No one believes a liar.

THE GRASSHOPPER AND THE ANTS

All summer long a merry grasshopper spent his days making music. When he saw the ants marching past him in a line, carrying seeds and grain to store in their hill, he laughed at their toil. "How foolish, to work so hard in the hot sun!" the grasshopper cried. "Summer's the time to play and sing. There's time enough to worry about winter when the first snow falls."

But when the days grew short and the first snow fell, the grasshopper could find nothing to eat. Shivering in the cold, he came to ask the ants for help. "Please, can't you spare me a seed or a leaf?" he begged. "I'm too hungry even to sing!"

The ants shrugged in disdain. "We worked hard for our food and we have none to spare," they said. "All summer long you made nothing but music. Now all winter long you can dance!"

Don't put off for tomorrow what you should do today.

THE STAG AND HIS REFLECTION

In the cool of the evening, a stag came to a clearing in the woods where there was a deep, still pool. Bending down, he caught sight of his own reflection in the quiet water.

"How strong and beautiful my antlers are," he thought. "But my legs–how thin and ugly they look. I'm embarrassed to be seen!"

As the stag looked away in shame, he heard hounds baying in the distance, and he knew that hunters were approaching. He bounded toward the woods, but as he ducked beneath the trees, his antlers became ensnared in some low branches.

"These cursed antlers have made me easy prey for the hunters and their dogs," he thought in despair. But after much kicking and struggling, his strong legs finally helped him to break free of his trap and quickly carried him to safety.

We often despise the thing that might save us.

THE CAT, THE ROOSTER, AND THE MOUSE

A young mouse begged his mother to let him take his first look at the world outside the mouse hole. "Very well," she answered, "but don't stay long, and come back and tell me everything you see."

The little mouse had not been gone five minutes, when he came dashing back into the mouse hole as fast as he could run. "My dear, whatever happened?" asked his mother.

"Oh, Mother," said the little mouse, trembling all over, "there are such strange creatures out there! First I saw a pretty animal, with soft striped fur and yellow eyes. When she saw me she waved her long tail as if she were glad to see me. But then I saw the most terrible monster! His head was all red, and his feet had long claws. And when he saw me, he opened up his mouth and let out a horrible shriek of 'Cock-a-doodle-do!' I ran away as fast as I could!"

"My dear," said his mother, "that pretty creature you saw was a cat, and she likes to eat young mice like you for dinner. And that terrible monster was nothing but a rooster, who only eats seeds and grain. Next time you go out, be more careful, and remember never to judge others by their looks."

Appearances can be deceiving.

THE NORTH WIND AND THE SUN

Of everything in the sky–the sun and the stars, the rain and the snow–the North Wind boasted that he was the strongest. "There is nothing that can resist me!" the North Wind cried, blowing such a blast that roofs lost their shingles and streams turned to ice.

"Are you sure?" asked the Sun. "The sky and the land are full of strong things. Why, it might even be that *I* am stronger than you!"

"You?" roared the North Wind, and laughed an icy laugh.

"Yes, why not? Let's put it to the test!" answered the Sun. "Do you see that traveler down below us? I'm sure I can make him take off his cloak. Are you strong enough to do the same?"

"Of course!" blustered the North Wind. He sent howling blasts of frigid air to tear the cloak away from the traveler. But the man, shivering in the cold, only wrapped the cloak tighter around himself. No gust that the North Wind blew could rip it from his grasp.

"Now it is my turn," said the Sun. And he sent warm beams of light down to where the traveler was walking. The man sighed with relief and pushed his cloak back off his shoulders. Steadily the Sun shone, until the traveler pulled off his hat, wiped the sweat from his forehead, and at last took off his cloak and lay down to rest in the shade of a nearby tree.

Gentle persuasion succeeds where force fails.

THE HEIFER AND THE OX

On the same farm there lived a foolish young heifer and a sturdy old ox. While the ox toiled in the fields, the heifer grazed happily in a lush green meadow. One day, as the ox came trudging past pulling a heavy plow, she called out to him, "My friend, I pity you! It must be terrible to work so hard. Don't you wish you could live as I do, without a care in the world?"

"Everything has its reasons," answered the old ox. "And I am well content with my lot in life."

The very next day the farmer spent the morning brushing the heifer, cleaning her hooves, and stringing garlands of flowers around her neck. "Look, my friend," she called to the ox, "don't you envy me now?"

"Let's wait and see what the day holds," replied the ox.

When the farmer had finished grooming the heifer, he led her to market. Several strangers immediately took notice. "What a lovely animal!" one of them said. "She will make a fine meal for our feast tonight!"

"Oh, no!" wailed the heifer. "The ox was right. I would rather have felt the yoke on my neck than the knife!"

Better a long life of toil than a short one of ease.

THE TORTOISE AND THE HARE

A conceited hare boasted about her speed to everyone who would listen. "Not even the North Wind is as fast as I am!" she declared. "No animal in the forest could beat me in a race!"

Now, a tortoise nearby grew tired of such bragging. "We've all heard you talk, but we've never seen you run," she said. "Why don't you race with me, and then we'll see who is the fastest."

The hare burst out laughing. "I could beat you standing still!" she exclaimed. But she agreed that they would race to an oak tree around a bend in the road. In an instant they were off–the hare soon out of sight, the tortoise plodding step by patient step.

"I've practically won already!" thought the hare as she dashed around the bend in the road. "I could stretch out here and take a little rest, and still beat that tortoise by a mile." And she settled down by the side of the road. She planned to jump up and finish the race the minute she saw the tortoise. But the grass was so soft and the sun was so warm that before the hare realized it, she had fallen fast asleep.

Meanwhile, the tortoise continued on. Slowly she came around the bend in the road and passed the sleeping hare. She was only a few feet from the oak tree when the hare woke from her nap.

Seeing the tortoise so close to the finish, the hare leaped up and tore along the road as if the hounds were after her. But she was too late. Before she could reach the oak tree, the tortoise had already been declared winner by the crowd of cheering bystanders.

Slow and steady wins the race.

THE DONKEY AND THE LAPDOG

A farmer had a little dog that he kept constantly by his side. The farmer also had a donkey, who lived in a warm stable and got plenty of fresh grain and sweet hay. But the donkey was not satisfied with his lot.

"I slave all day, hauling wood or pulling the cart to market," the donkey grumbled. "And then I'm shut in the stable, while that dog sleeps on the master's lap and eats from his plate!" Perhaps, he thought, if he behaved like the dog, his master would reward him with the same life of ease.

That very night, the donkey crept out of the stable and into the house where the farmer sat at supper. "First I'll frisk about and chase my tail, just as the dog does," thought the donkey. And he danced about the room, flinging up his hooves until the table toppled over and dishes went flying.

"Now I'll sit on his lap!" said the donkey to himself, and he put his heavy hooves up on the master's chair.

"Help! Save me from this mad beast!" bellowed the terrified farmer. His servants came running and, with shouts and blows, drove the donkey back to the stable.

"I suppose I'm a fine donkey," the donkey lamented, "but I'll never be a lapdog!"

What's right for one may be wrong for another.

THE WOLF IN SHEEP'S CLOTHING

A hungry wolf had been stalking a flock of sheep for many days when he came upon a worn-out sheepskin. Delighted, he devised a plan to outwit the flock's watchful shepherd.

The wolf slunk into the fold one night, covered in a sheepskin disguise. In the dark the shepherd saw nothing amiss. "Aha!" thought the wolf. "As soon as the shepherd goes to bed, I'll eat as many sheep as I please!"

But it just so happened that the shepherd had a taste for fresh mutton that night. Thinking only of his supper, the shepherd seized hold of the nearest sheep to ready it for slaughter–and found himself holding the wolf!

"What do you think you're doing in my flock?" the astonished man cried, and raised his knife high. "Rest assured, this is the last time I'll find you lurking here!"

Tricks often put the trickster in peril.

THE LARK AND HER CHILDREN

A lark made her nest in a field of young wheat. By the time her eggs hatched, the wheat had grown straight and tall. All summer long the wheat ripened and grew golden while the young birds grew in size and strength.

The fledglings were nearly ready to leave the nest when they heard the farmer talking to his sons. "The wheat's ripened at last," he said. "We'll call our friends and neighbors in to help us harvest it."

The little birds were frightened that their nest might be destroyed, and when their mother returned to the nest that night, they told her what they'd overheard. "Never fear, my children," the lark replied. "We still have some time left. Practice your flying and make sure your wings are strong."

A few days later the young larks once again heard the farmer talking. "That wheat must be harvested at once," he said. "We can't wait any longer for help from our friends. Tomorrow we'll set to work ourselves."

When her children told the lark what the farmer had said, she answered, "Then it's time for us to be gone. For once a man is ready to do his own work, there will be no more delay."

If you want something done, do it yourself.

THE MICE AND THE WEASELS

The mice who lived in a certain wood were in constant fear of the weasels, who hunted them for food. At last the mice held a council and decided to declare war on their enemies. "But friends, listen to me!" cried one mouse. "To be a real army we will need commanders to lead us." Mice on all sides clamored for the honor, and the bravest were chosen by vote. And the mouse who had been clever enough to suggest that an army needed leaders was made the general.

Then this mouse spoke up again. "It's only right that all the officers should wear uniforms, so no one will mistake us for common soldiers," he suggested. Everyone agreed, and the mice fashioned tall

straw helmets for the commanders to wear. The general's helmet was crowned with bright red plumes.

The mouse general sent a challenge to the weasels, and soon the day of battle came. The mouse army hid themselves in the tall grass, planning to ambush their enemies. But the weasels easily spotted the plume of the general's helmet waving above the grass, and they pounced. Shrieking in terror, the mice ran for their lives.

The general fled with the rest, but when he dived headfirst for his hole, his straw helmet was too big to fit inside. The common soldiers managed to dash to safety, but the general and all his commanders were devoured.

Don't sacrifice what is practical for the sake of pomp and show.

THE BOY AND THE ALMONDS

A hungry boy eyed a jar of almonds sitting on the kitchen table. "Mother, please, can I have some nuts?" he asked, his mouth watering.

"Take one handful, but no more," said his mother. "It's almost supper time."

Greedily the boy grabbed as many almonds as he could hold. But his bulging fist wouldn't fit back through the mouth of the jar. Though the boy tugged and twisted until his whole arm ached, he could not get his hand free.

"My dear," his mother said, "if you don't let go of half the nuts you have, you won't be able to eat any. Take a few now, and you may have some more after dinner is over."

A little at a time is better than none at all.

THE STORK AND THE CRANES

A flock of cranes saw a lone stork nesting in a tree. "Come with us," they called as they flew by. "We're going to a field where there is tender grain to eat, as much as you can hold!"

Eagerly, the hungry stork flew with the cranes to the field. But before any of the birds had so much as taken a bite, a farmer crept up behind them and threw a heavy net over them all.

"Oh, please," cried the stork, "let me go! I'm a stork, you see, not a crane like the rest. I don't belong with this flock!"

"You may be innocent," replied the farmer, "but you kept company with thieves, and now you'll share their punishment as well."

You are judged by the company you keep.

ANDROCLES AND THE LION

Androcles was a slave who suffered under a cruel and vicious master. Although Androcles worked from sunrise to sunset, his master gave him scarcely enough food to live on, and had him beaten time and time again. At last Androcles made up his mind to run away into the woods. "Even if I'm killed by wild beasts," he thought, "it would be better than this." And he slipped away into the forest.

When night was about to fall, a strange sound suddenly reached his ears–a moaning and whimpering as if one nearby were in pain. As he peered around the trees, he gasped and stood frozen in the shadow of the trees–for what he saw was a lion!

The lion was licking his paw with his great tongue and gnawing at it with his sharp teeth. Looking closer, Androcles saw that a long, sharp thorn had buried itself deep in the lion's paw. "Why, it's hurt," he thought with pity, forgetting his fear.

Careful not to alarm the animal, Androcles crept toward the lion. He gently took hold of the injured paw, pulled the thorn out, and then bound up the wound with a bandage torn from his cloak.

The lion licked Androcles' hand in gratitude, and from that moment on they were friends. Every day the lion went hunting and brought back fresh meat for Androcles to eat, and every night Androcles slept safely in the lion's den.

But one day, as the lion was out in the forest, he was trapped by a band of hunters. And that same day, Androcles was captured by some soldiers who were passing through the forest. As punishment for running away from his master, Androcles was taken to the city, where he was to be thrown to the lions. When the day of Androcles' execution arrived, even the emperor came to the crowded arena to watch.

The soldiers dragged Androcles into the arena and left him there. "What a wretched life!" Androcles thought in despair. "Those days I spent in the forest with the lion were the only time I was happy."

Then the soldiers released the lion. Androcles shut his eyes in dread, expecting to be torn limb from limb. But no tooth or claw touched him. When Androcles opened his eyes in amazement, he saw his own lion crouched happily at his feet. Androcles laughed with joy as he knelt to embrace his friend.

Much astonished, the emperor called out, "Who is this slave who can tame lions?" Androcles rose and bowed to the emperor.

"My lord," he said, "I was able to do this lion a kindness, and he has repaid me with greater loyalty than I ever found in the world of women and men." And he told the emperor his story.

Impressed with Androcles courage and compassion, the emperor pardoned him and set him free. Androcles and the lion returned to the forest, where they lived happily together the rest of their days.

Gratitude is not limited to humankind.

THE DONKEY'S SHADOW

A traveler who had to cross a desert plain hired a donkey to carry him on the journey, and offered the donkey's owner a good sum to act as a guide. They set out early in the morning, the traveler riding on the donkey and his guide walking alongside. Soon they had left all greenery behind, and as the sun rose higher in the sky, the heat scorched their skins and parched their throats.

At last the traveler called a halt. Since there was no other shade, he threw himself down to rest in the donkey's shadow.

"What right do you have to that shade?" protested the guide. "Move over–that's my place to rest."

"Cheat!" answered the traveler angrily. "Didn't I pay you for the use of the donkey all day long?"

"You paid me for the donkey, it's true," retorted the guide, "but you never paid for his shadow!"

As they argued, neither remembered to keep hold of the donkey's reins. Frightened by the shouting, the donkey took to his heels and ran off across the desert, leaving the two men with no shade to rest in and no beast to ride.

We lose what really matters when we quarrel over something worthless.

THE FOX AND THE GOAT

One hot day a fox happened upon a deep well. Longing for a drink, he leaned too far over the edge and tumbled in headfirst.

Seeing no way out, the fox sat mournfully at the bottom of the well. Soon he saw a goat poke his head over the edge. "My goodness, friend Fox, whatever are you doing down there?" asked the goat in astonishment.

The crafty fox called up, "Oh, I'm just enjoying this delicious water–so sweet! Aren't you thirsty, friend Goat? Why don't you come down?"

At once the foolish goat jumped down beside the fox. "Ah, wonderful," he said after drinking his fill. "But now, how do we get out of this well?"

"I know how *I'll* get out," replied the fox. Nimbly he leaped onto the goat's back, hopped onto his horns, and scrambled out of the well.

"Wait!" cried the goat. "What about me?"

"If you had brains in your head instead of a beard on your chin," the fox replied, "you never would have jumped in to begin with. Now find your own way out!"

Look before you leap.

THE MISER

A man loved gold so dearly that he sold all his possessions for a bag of gold coins bigger than a ram's head. He buried the gold in his garden, and every day he went to dig it up and count each and every piece of the precious metal.

But one day a thief saw him at this, and that very night came and dug up the gold for himself. When the miser discovered the empty hole the next morning, his wails could be heard far and wide.

A young servant boy came running to see the trouble. "Sir," he said, "there's no need to weep. Here, replace your gold with this." And he handed his master a large, heavy rock.

"This isn't gold, you fool!" raged the miser, but the boy shrugged.

"You never meant to spend the gold, master, so what does it matter?" he asked. "That rock is just as much use to you as those coins ever were!"

Something we never use is worthless.

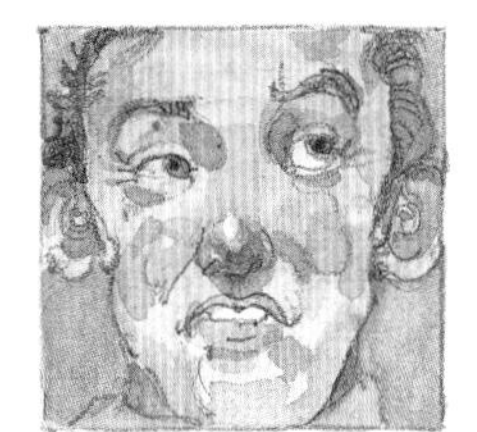

THE TROUBLESOME DOG

A farmer had a troublesome dog who chased the chickens, frightened the sheep, and dug up the vegetable garden. So the exasperated farmer tied a collar with a heavy brass bell around the dog's neck, to warn everyone of his presence.

The foolish dog thought the bell was something very fine. "Look at what the farmer gave me," he boasted. He pranced about the farmyard, setting the bell ringing. "No one else on the farm has a bell like mine!" he called out proudly.

"That's because no one else causes half as much trouble as you do!" scolded a wise old dog. "If you had some sense, you'd hide that bell. Don't you know it only proves what a poor excuse for a dog you are?"

Notoriety is not fame.

THE MILKMAID AND HER PAIL

A milkmaid was walking down the road, balancing on her head a bucket full of fresh, sweet milk. And as she walked, she was busy daydreaming.

"Milk this rich," she thought, "will surely give plenty of cream. I'll churn the cream into fresh white butter, and I'll take the butter to market. After I sell it, I'll buy a dozen eggs, and soon I'll have a dozen chickens running around the yard. I'll sell the chickens for a good price, and with the money I'll buy myself a new dress–a green one with lace, to wear to the fair in the summer. And when the miller's son sees me in that dress, he'll beg to dance with me. But will I let him? Never! When he asks me, I'll just toss my head–like this!"

As the milkmaid tossed her head in scorn, her wooden bucket fell to the ground and split in two. And so the milkmaid had nothing–no dress, no chickens, no eggs, no butter, not even the milk she had to start with.

Don't count your chickens before they're hatched.

THE PIG AND THE SHEEP

When a shepherd came to count his sheep one morning, he was thunderstruck to find a pig huddled among his flock. "However he came to be here, that pig will fetch a fat price at the butcher's!" the shepherd thought. And he snatched up the pig and tucked him snugly under one arm.

At once the pig began to squeal and kick, thrashing his short legs. "What a fuss you're making!" scolded one elderly sheep. "The shepherd often carries one of us away, but you'd never see a sheep whimper like that. Show a little courage!"

"Easy for you to say!" gasped the frightened pig. "When the shepherd carries you away, he only wants your wool. But he wants *my* bacon, and that will be the end of me!"

It's easy to talk of courage when you're safe and sound.

THE ROOSTERS AND THE EAGLE

Two roosters who lived on the same farm constantly quarreled over who was lord of the yard. Finally, they agreed to settle the matter by combat. Bright feathers flew and dust swirled in clouds. At last one of the roosters begged for his life to be spared.

The victor flew to the top of the henhouse and let out a loud, triumphant crow. "I am the king!" he proclaimed. But an eagle who was soaring overhead heard him. With a sudden swoop the eagle dived down, snatched the rooster in his claws, and carried him away.

Pride goes before a fall.

THE MILLER, HIS SON, AND THEIR DONKEY

A miller and his son set out to market to sell their donkey, leading the beast behind them. They had not gotten far down the road when they passed a group of schoolgirls. "Look, what fools!" mocked one laughing girl. "Why are they walking on such a hot day, when at least one of them could ride?"

"It's worth a try," said the miller thoughtfully. He lifted his young son up onto the donkey's back, and they continued on their way.

Soon after, they came across three farmers who stood by the side of the road. "It's just as I said!" one of the three exclaimed as the miller and his son went by. "There's no respect for age these days. Look at that lazy boy riding at his ease, while his poor father walks in the dust!"

"He may be right," said the miller. His son climbed off the donkey's back and the miller himself got on.

They had not gone much farther when they passed an old woman with a basket of apples. "For shame!" she scolded. "How can you ride in comfort, old man, while that poor boy can hardly keep up?"

"It's true!" said the miller. He helped his son to mount the donkey behind him.

Not a mile further, they passed a wealthy merchant on horseback. "Why, friend!" the merchant called out, laughing. "How can the two of you ride on that poor skinny beast? You could carry him more easily than he can carry you!"

"That's the answer!" said the miller. He and his son got down from the donkey and cut a long branch from a tree. Tying the donkey's feet together, they slung him from the pole, heaved the wood over their shoulders, and staggered once more toward the town.

As the miller and his son came to the bridge just outside the town walls, a crowd gathered, laughing at the ridiculous sight. Frightened by the noise, the donkey began to kick and thrash. The pole creaked and bent under his weight until it broke with a snap, and the poor donkey tumbled off the bridge into the water.

The miller and his son were forced to turn again for home, without the money they had hoped to make, and without the donkey they had before.

If you try and please everyone, you'll please no one–not even yourself.

THE FOX AND THE PHEASANTS

Several pheasants were perched on a tree limb when they saw a fox down below. "Keep your eye on him!" one of them whispered to the rest. "We're safe up here, but you know how cunning foxes can be!"

The pheasants huddled together and peered down at the fox, who began to prance about as though he had gone suddenly mad. He leaped and jumped; he pawed the air; he shook his tail as though a spark had landed on it. The pheasants began to laugh at the fox's antics. At last the fox began to twirl in a circle. Faster and faster he went, until the bemused pheasants grew dizzy watching him. Their heads spinning, they lost their balance and fell to the ground.

Quick as thought, the fox snapped up two or three birds. "Thank you for watching!" he said, with a little bow.

Danger often comes when we feel safe.

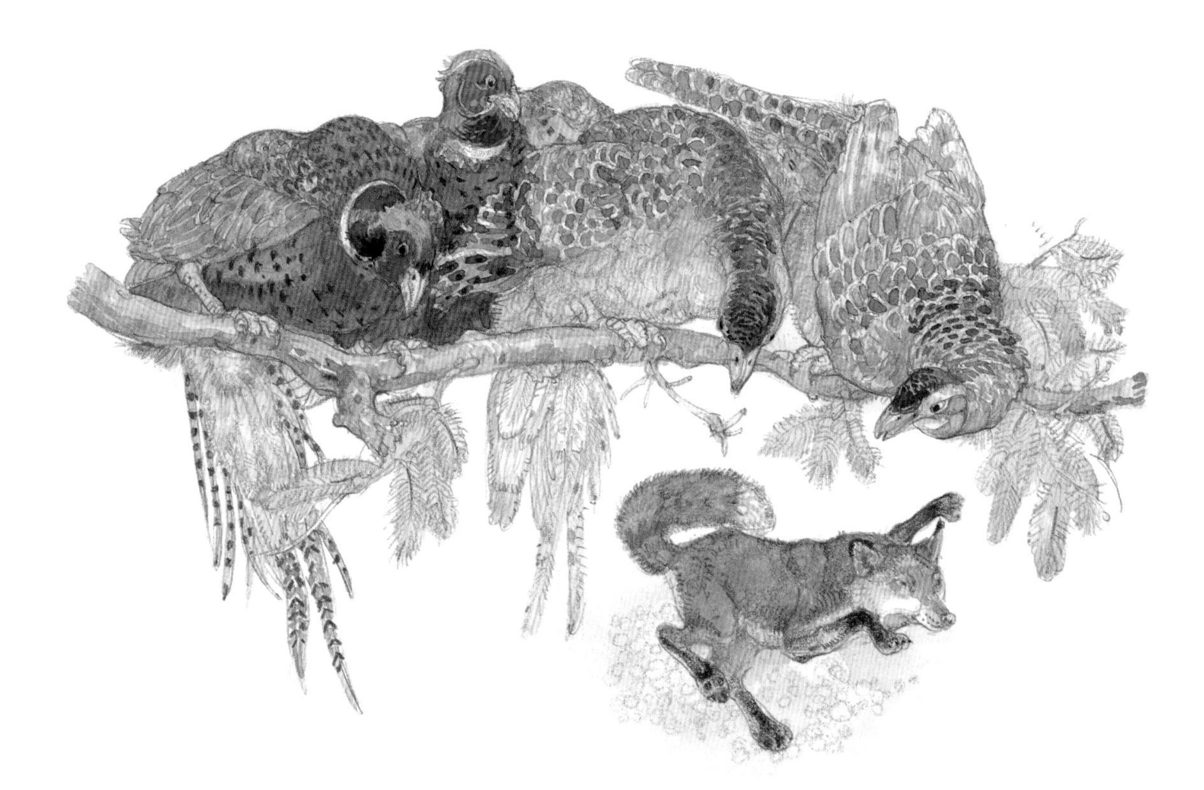

THE LION AND THE MOUSE

One day while a mouse was creeping through the tall grass, she happened upon a great lion asleep in the sun. "I might see for quite a long distance from the top of that beast's back," she thought. Boldly the mouse crept up the lion's flank and scampered along his spine.

The tickling of the mouse's tiny feet woke the lion. With one swipe he snatched her in his claws and dangled her by her tail in front of his nose. "For daring to interrupt my nap," the lion growled, "you'll be my next meal!"

"Oh, please," the terrified mouse gasped, "let me go, and I promise one day I'll help you in return."

The lion shook with laughter. "Impossible!" he roared. But the proud animal was so amused by the idea that he allowed the mouse to go.

Not long after, the lion was caught in a trap set by some clever hunters. No matter how the powerful beast thrashed and fought, he could not free himself from the strong net that raised him from the ground. No other animal dared come near to help for fear of the hunters. But when the brave little mouse heard his cries, she remembered her promise and hurried to his side. Quickly she gnawed through the sturdy ropes with her sharp teeth until the lion could escape to freedom.

"You see," she said, "there are times when even a tiny mouse can help a lion."

Even the strongest can sometimes use the help of the smallest.

THE OXEN AND THE WAGON WHEELS

One rainy day a pair of oxen pulled a cart down a country lane. The dirt of the road had turned to muck and mire, and the oxen trudged through mud up to their knees, straining against the weight of the cart with every step. Still, they never uttered one word of complaint.

The wheels of the cart, on the other hand, groaned with every turn and creaked at every jolt. At last the oxen could endure it no longer.

"Keep quiet!" they cried. "You have only to turn; what is that to grumble over? We have to pull all the weight of the cart, and you don't hear us complaining!"

Those who complain most often suffer least.

THE DOG IN THE MANGER

A dog found a cozy spot to sleep, curled up in the soft hay of the oxen's manger. When the oxen came into the stables, tired from plowing the field and eager for their supper, the dog bared his teeth and growled at them, as if the manger were filled with the best of meat and bones all for himself.

"Selfish beast!" one of them exclaimed, not daring to come near. "He can't eat the hay himself, yet he still won't give any to us who are so hungry for it!"

Don't grudge others what you cannot enjoy yourself.

THE GNAT AND THE BULL

A gnat flew busily through a meadow full of wildflowers. Halfway across, he saw a great bull peacefully grazing. "I'll just take a moment's rest on one of his horns," the gnat thought, and settled down for a few minutes.

Then, buzzing anxiously in the bull's ear, the gnat said, "Pardon me, sir. I'll be leaving now, for I've many important things to see to. But I hope my weight has not inconvenienced you terribly."

"Why, not at all," replied the bull calmly. "I never even knew you were there."

We are rarely as important as we think we are.

THE FOX AND THE STORK

A fox was jealous of his neighbor the stork for her elegance and grace. He longed to find a way to make her look foolish, and at last he had an idea. "My dear friend," he said, hiding his cunning with gracious manners, "would you be so kind as to join me for dinner?"

"Why, I'd love to," replied the stork.

But when the stork arrived at the fox's house, all he served her was a thin broth in a shallow bowl. The hungry stork could only wet the tip of her long bill, while the fox lapped up his dinner eagerly. But the stork didn't complain, for she was hatching a plan of her own. "What a delicious dinner!" she said politely. "You must dine with me tomorrow, good neighbor."

When the fox arrived at the stork's house the next day, he smelled a delicious fish soup. He licked his lips eagerly. But when he got to the table, the soup was served in a tall glass jar with a narrow neck. With her long bill, the stork drank her soup easily, but the fox could only lick a few drops from around the neck of the jar.

"What is this?" he growled. "I can't eat this, and you know it!"

"My dear friend," replied the stork calmly, "I'm sure you will enjoy this dinner just as much as I enjoyed the one you served to me."

Do unto others as you would have them do unto you.

THE WOLF AND THE HOUSE DOG

A wolf who lived in the forest fell on hard times, and could barely catch enough food to keep from starving. Soon her ribs were showing through her coat, and she could hardly sleep at night for hunger.

One day the wolf happened to meet a sleek, plump dog from the village. Puzzled, the wolf looked him over and exclaimed, "How is it that you appear to be so well-fed, when game has been so scarce?"

"I never have to hunt for game," boasted the dog. "My master feeds me meat from his own plate, and the servants give me scraps from the kitchen every day. All I have to do is bark at every stranger that comes near and keep watch over the house by night."

The wolf could hardly believe her ears. "If I find a family to take me in," she asked, "will they treat me the same way?"

“No doubt of it!” the dog replied. “Just come along with me and I’ll find you a place.” Eagerly the wolf trotted beside the dog. But as they left the shadow of the trees, the wolf saw something near the dog’s neck flash in the bright sunlight.

“Pardon me, but what is that around your neck?” she asked.

“Oh, nothing,” said the dog. “It’s just the ring on my collar where they fasten me to the chain.”

“Chain!” cried the wolf in horror, stopping in her tracks.

“Of course,” said the dog. “They chain us up at night, so we won’t run away.” The dog looked over his shoulder. “Why did you stop, Wolf? Aren’t you coming?”

“Certainly not,” said the wolf. “You may go back to your master, if you will. But I’d rather starve to death in the woods than eat one meal with a chain around my neck.”

Lean freedom is better than fat slavery.

THE FOX AND THE GRAPES

Walking along a dry and dusty road, a fox glanced up and saw a bunch of ripe purple grapes growing over his head. They were plump and looked ready to burst with juice, and a breeze brought their sweet scent to the fox’s keen nose. He wanted to taste those plump grapes more than anything.

The fox jumped as high as he could, but the grapes hung just beyond his reach. He took a running start and jumped even higher, but still he fell short. Again and again he tried, but in vain.

“Those grapes don’t look very ripe,” he said to himself finally. “They’re just small and green. Not worth bothering about. Why should I waste my time on a bunch of sour grapes?”

And with his head held high the fox walked off down the road.

It’s easy to scorn what you cannot reach.

THE GOOSE AND THE GOLDEN EGGS

Once there was a poor farmer who welcomed any creatures that strayed onto his land. One day a strange new goose appeared among his birds; and when he and his wife came to feed her the next morning, they were amazed to find a gleaming golden egg in her nest of straw. Every morning after that it was the same: the goose laid another egg of solid gold.

Soon the farmer and his wife were richer than they had ever dreamed of being. But still they wanted more. "One egg a day isn't nearly enough," the farmer complained.

"If we cut that goose open, we'll get all the eggs at once!" his wife declared.

But when they had killed the goose, they found not one egg inside her. "What have we done?" the farmer's wife mourned. "Once we dressed in silks and velvets and ate fine food off silver plates, but now we're just poor farmers again."

Those who want everything may end up with nothing.

THE SHEPHERD AND THE WILD GOATS

A shepherd was out with his goats on a mountainside when a fierce storm blew in. He drove the animals into a nearby cave for shelter, and found that a flock of wild goats had taken refuge there as well.

"If I feed these wild goats," thought the shepherd, "then perhaps they'll stay with me. In no time at all my flock will double in size!"

So the shepherd gave the wild goats the best of his grain and hay, and made sure they had fresh water to drink. But since he had only a little food with him, he gave his own goats no more than a few handfuls of grain.

When the storm finally passed, the wild goats bounded out of the cave without a backward glance. "Wait!" cried the shepherd angrily. "Is this the thanks I get for taking care of you?"

One of the wild goats looked back. "We saw how you treated your own flock," she answered. "Why should we think you'd treat us any differently if we stayed with you?"

Don't neglect old friends for new ones.

THE BUNDLE OF STICKS

An old farmer had three sons who quarreled among themselves from dawn till dusk. One day, the farmer fell gravely ill. Wishing to make peace among his sons before he died, he called them to his bedside and asked them to bring a thick bundle of sticks.

"Can you break these in two?" asked the farmer, handing the sticks to his oldest son.

"Of course!" the young man answered scornfully. But even though he tried until he was red in the face, he couldn't break the bundle of sticks.

"Why, those sticks are no thicker than my finger," mocked the second son.

"I could break those sticks like straw," boasted the third. And they both tried with all their might, but neither could break the bundle of sticks in two.

Then the father drew three sticks from the bundle and handed one to each of his sons. "Can you break them now?" he asked. And they did so easily.

"Let the sticks teach you," said the father to his sons, "how strong you are when you are allied together, and how easily you can be broken on your own."

In unity there is strength.

KING LOG AND KING STORK

A band of frogs lived a carefree life, splashing about their small pond. They had warm rocks to bask on and plenty of tasty flies to eat. But when some of the older frogs got together, they began to grumble.

"There's no discipline or order," they complained. "All the frogs do just as they please!" So the frogs asked the Sun to send them a king to rule over them.

The Sun became irritated that the foolish frogs didn't see how lucky they were. "Here is your king!" he declared, and threw a heavy log down into their pond. It fell with a mighty splash.

The frightened frogs dived beneath the water and hid behind the rocks. "Truly this is a great king!" they whispered among themselves.

One brave frog dared to approach the floating log. "Welcome to our pond, O great King Log," he said. But the log made no reply.

One by one, the other curious frogs crept out to see King Log. No matter what they said or did to it, the log made no response. Before long the young frogs were diving off King Log into the water.

"This king is worth nothing," one of them objected. "He never even speaks!" And they all asked the Sun to send them another king, one who would govern them sternly and well.

When he saw the frogs again refusing to be content, the Sun grew angry. "Very well, you shall have what you ask for!" he said. And he sent them down a new king–a hungry stork.

King Stork pounced on the frogs and began gobbling them up two or three at a time. The frogs fled for their lives, begging the Sun to take this terrible king away from them.

"You asked for a king, and now you have one!" answered the Sun. And for many years the frogs lived in misery under King Stork's rule.

Don't change better for worse.

THE DONKEY AND THE LOAD OF SALT

A wealthy merchant bought many baskets of salt, and tied them on his donkey to carry them to market. On the way, as they crossed a shallow river, the donkey slipped beneath his heavy load and fell into the water. By the time he scrambled to his feet again, half the salt in the baskets had been washed away.

The merchant cursed at the loss. But the donkey was pleased to discover that the baskets were only half as heavy as before. And he cheerfully carried his lightened load to market.

At the market, the merchant sold what was left of his salt and bought several bags of sponges. Tying them on the donkey's back, he set out again for home. When they came to the river, the donkey thought of what happened on his way to the market. He pretended to slip and rolled into the water, hoping his load would be lightened.

But the sponges were not washed away. Instead, they soaked up water until they swelled fat and heavy. The merchant drove the donkey to his feet again, and the beast staggered home under a load twice as heavy as before.

The method should suit the circumstances.

THE PEACOCK'S TAIL

There was a time when the peacock could fly higher than any other bird, over the trees and nearly up to the sunlit clouds. One day after soaring above the earth, the peacock landed near a quiet pool and glimpsed his reflection in the water. Horrified, he saw that his feathers were dull brown–without a single scarlet plume or golden crest among them. "This is terrible!" he cried. "I would pay any price if only I could be beautiful." And he fell asleep that night still lamenting his plainness.

When he woke the next morning, he found that his wish had been granted. His dull feathers had been transformed to shimmering blue and emerald green, purple and turquoise. And he was most delighted with the very long tail that he could spread out behind him like an emperor's fan. The peacock strolled through the woods, showing off his glorious feathers to every bird he met.

But even this wasn't enough. "Everyone must see me!" the vain bird thought. "I'll fly high above the trees, and show my new feathers to all." When he stretched out his wings, however, he found that the weight of his heavy tail pinned him to the ground.

A small brown sparrow who sat in a tree above saw the peacock struggling to fly. "You have what you wanted," he called down. "But is beauty worth such a price?" And before the peacock could reply, the sparrow spread his wings and soared away.

Vanity carries a heavy price.

THE MAN AND THE LION

A man and a lion happened to meet on the road, and fell into conversation. It wasn't long before they began to argue.

"Any fool knows that a lion is stronger than a man," the lion boasted. "A lion is the King of the Beasts!"

"He may be, but a man is mightier yet, and everybody knows it!" proclaimed the man. "Just look at that statue over there!" And he pointed to a tall marble statue by the roadside, showing a man gripping a lion by the throat.

"That proves nothing," protested the lion. "After all, a man carved that statue! It would have been quite a different scene had a lion made it!"

There are two sides to every story.

THE FISHERMAN AND HIS CATCH

A hardworking fisherman had bad luck one day on the water and caught only a single, small fish. "You're barely big enough for a mouthful!" he exclaimed. "But at least you'll be something to bring home to my family for dinner."

The little fish gasped. "Have mercy and spare my life! You can see what a pitiful meal I'd make. If you throw me back, I promise I'll grow into a fish it would truly be worth your while to catch!"

But the fisherman put the fish in his basket, and began rowing for home. "You may be small," he said, "but if I throw you back now, I may never catch you again."

A small gain today is better than a large promise for tomorrow.

THE ASTROLOGER

A man learned to observe the movements of the stars in order to predict the future. He soon became famous as an astrologer, and people traveled from miles around to pay for his advice.

One evening this man was walking along the road, his eyes fixed on the heavens and what great fortune he saw there. But meanwhile he paid no heed to the path, and before he knew it he had tumbled head over heels into a pit of muddy water.

His neighbors heard his shouts and came running. But when they saw who had fallen into the hole they had no pity. "He can predict the future, but he couldn't foresee this!" one of them cried.

And another, helping the man up, told him, "You'd better spend less time watching the stars, and more time watching your feet!"

Don't neglect small things when thinking of great ones.

THE HORSE AND THE STAG

Long ago, when the horse and the stag lived together in the forest, they argued and fought over who had the right to graze on the most tender meadow grass or drink at the sweetest pools. Over the years, they came to be openly at war.

The horse went to a man who lived near the edge of the forest, and proposed an alliance. "Help me defeat the stag," she told him, "and one day I'll do you a favor in return."

"Very well," said the man. "But you must let me put this saddle on your back and this bridle over your head, or I won't be able to help you."

The horse agreed, and together they went in search of the stag. When the stag saw the man riding on the horse, he fled in terror, for the man and his dogs had often hunted him before.

The horse neighed in triumph. "Thank you, good friend. I will never forget your kindness. And now, will you please take off this saddle and bridle?"

But the man simply laughed. "You were a fool to let me harness you in the first place," he said. "You won't get them off so easily now!"

And the horse, suffering under the bit and spur, had to serve the man for the rest of her days.

Revenge often carries too high a price.

THE TOWN MOUSE AND THE COUNTRY MOUSE

A mouse who lived in the country invited her cousin from the town for dinner. The country mouse worked all day to prepare the dinner, gathering a few peas, a stalk of barley, a crust of bread, and cold water in a green leaf to drink. When the town mouse arrived, the humble country mouse set all the best food before her guest.

The town mouse ate a few of the peas and tasted a bite of the bread, trying her best to be polite. But at last she turned to her cousin and said, "My dear, how can you live like this? Ants and worms eat better food! Come with me to the city, and I'll show you how a mouse should live."

That very night the country mouse went with her cousin to a grand mansion in the heart of the city. The two mice crept into the dining room, where the remains of a banquet were still spread on the table. "Look at all the good things here!" the town mouse said proudly. "Try a little honey on your bread! Have some of the cheese, it's delicious!"

The country mouse gazed about her in wonder. But just as she prepared to take her first bite, there was a hiss and yowl, and a cat leaped onto the table. The two mice fled for their lives, and barely managed to dash into a hole in the wall.

"Don't worry," said her cousin. "The cat never stays for long, and we can soon finish our dinner. We'll be perfectly safe as long as the dog stays away."

"A cat and a dog!" cried the astounded country mouse. "My dear cousin, you may stay and enjoy your feast, but I'm going right back home where I can eat my crust of bread in peace."

Poverty in safety is better than riches in peril.

THE SICK LION

A lion who had lived many years found he could not hunt as well as he once did. He feared he would starve, until he came up with a plan to catch fresh meat.

He crawled into his cave and sent the crow to spread the news that King Lion had not long to live. "Tell them," he said to the crow, "that all must come to see me, for I have an important message to deliver to each before I die."

The deer was the first to come. But when she reached a dark corner of his cave, the lion leaped on her and devoured her. And when the wolf and later the rabbit arrived, he treated each the same way.

The fox had also heard the lion's message and hurried to his cave. But at the mouth of the cave he hesitated. From inside, the lion called out in a weak and quavering voice, "Is that you, my wise friend fox? Why don't you come in and pay your respects to your king?"

"Forgive me, King Lion," replied the fox. "But I see the footprints of the deer, the rabbit, and the wolf all entering your cave, and none coming out again. Surely it can't be good for your health to be in crowded quarters. Until someone leaves and there is more room, I think I'll wait out here."

Make sure there's a way out before you go in.

THE GARDENER AND HIS DOG

While a gardener was at work one day, his little dog chased a butterfly about the flower beds. Playfully she ran this way and that, paying no heed to where she was going, until she slipped and fell into a deep, cold well.

The gardener heard his dog's frightened barks and came quickly running. But when he reached out a hand to pull her to safety, the ungrateful animal growled and snapped at his fingers.

"Little beast!" the gardener cried. "I came to rescue you, and this is the thanks I get? Then stay in there until you find your own way out!"

Don't bite the hand that feeds you.

THE BOY WHO WENT SWIMMING

A boy who was walking by the river on a hot day could not resist the temptation to go for a swim. But the current was much fiercer than he expected. As he struggled to reach the shore again, the river swept him downstream toward some sharp, deadly rocks.

As he kicked and splashed, the boy spotted a man walking along the riverbank. "Help me!" he shouted.

"What a fool you are, to go swimming in that river!" scolded the man. "What would have happened if I hadn't come along? When I tell your parents what a risk you took, they'll give you such a hiding! Why, when I was a boy–"

"Please, sir!" the terrified boy cried out. "Save me now, and afterward you can lecture me as much as you please!"

There is a time and a place for everything.

THE TRAVELERS AND THE BEAR

Two men were traveling through the forest together on a lonely trail. Soon they heard a sound up ahead as if heavy feet were trampling through the underbrush.

"It could be a bear!" one whispered with alarm, and quickly as he could, he scrambled up a tall tree. He had barely reached the first branch when a huge brown bear thrust aside the bushes and stepped out onto the path.

Hugging the trunk with both arms, the first traveler refused to lend a hand to his terrified companion, who threw himself on the ground and prepared for death.

The bear lowered its great head and sniffed at the man, ruffling his hair with its nose. Then, to the amazement of both men, the fierce beast walked away.

The first traveler slid down from his tree. "Why, it almost looked as if the bear whispered something in your ear," he marveled.

"It did," said the second traveler. "It told me to chose a better companion for my next journey."

Misfortune is the true test of friendship.

THE FOX AND THE CROW

One morning a fox was trotting through the woods in search of a tasty morsel to eat. Looking up, she spied a crow perched in a tree overhead, with a large piece of cheese held tight in her beak.

"That cheese would be just the thing for my breakfast," thought the fox. And sitting down beneath the tree, she gazed up at the crow as if hypnotized by her beauty.

"Loveliest of creatures!" she called loudly. "Your feathers shine like silk, your wings are black as night! How bright your eyes glow! Oh, it's such a pity I've heard that you can't sing. If only you could sing just one note, you'd be the most perfect creature alive!"

The crow, hearing all this flattery, quickly grew vain. "Why, the fox is right–my feathers *are* beautiful, my eyes *do* glow!" she thought. "Not sing? Why surely I can sing, and better than any common bird in the forest!" And she opened up her mouth to let out a loud "*Caw, caw!*"

Down fell the cheese, and the fox snapped it up in two bites. "Thank you for my breakfast, friend!" she called. "I see you have a voice indeed, but where is your brain?"

Never trust flatterers.

THE WOLF AND THE CRANE

A wolf with a bone caught in his throat darted around the forest begging for help from every animal he saw. But, wary of his sharp fangs, none dared to come near. At last the gasping wolf called out desperately, "I promise a fine reward to anyone who will take this bone out of my throat!"

When the crane heard this, she stepped forward boldly, for everyone knew that the wolf was rich. The wolf opened his jaws wide while the crane gingerly pulled the bone free with her long bill.

"At last!" the wolf cried out in relief, and he turned to go.

"But have you forgotten my reward?" the crane called anxiously.

"What?" snarled the ungrateful wolf. "Isn't it enough that you put your head in a wolf's mouth and lived to tell the tale? Now, fly off before I decide to finish my meal by eating you!"

There's no reward for helping the wicked.

LITTLE CRAB AND HIS GRANDMOTHER

Grandmother Crab was quietly resting on the seabed when Little Crab scuttled by.

"Foolish child!" she scolded. "Why are you walking sideways like that? You should always march straight ahead, and show the world you're proud to be a crab!"

Now, Little Crab *was* proud to be a crab, and he wanted the world to know it. "Show me how, Grandmother," he cried, "and I'll never walk any other way!"

With great dignity, Grandmother Crab stood up. But when she took a step, she could only go sideways, just like Little Crab. And when she tried again, she tripped and fell with a thump to the ocean floor.

Grandmother Crab sat up stiffly. "On second thought, Little Crab," she said, "a true crab should always be very proud to walk sideways."

Master what you teach.

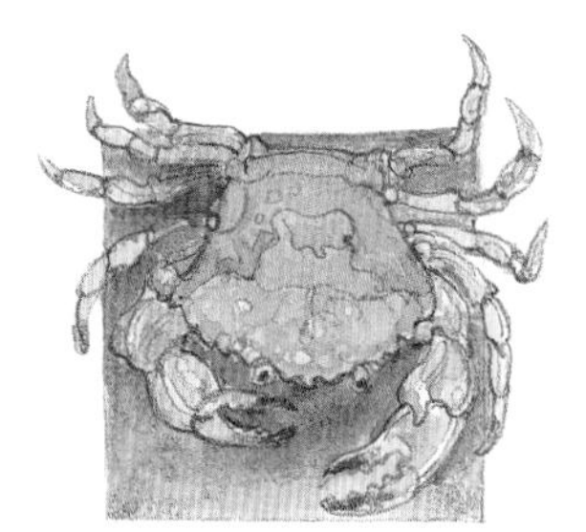

THE DONKEY IN THE LION'S SKIN

By chance a donkey came across a lion's skin lying in the bushes. "I'll put it on and pretend to be King Lion himself!" he declared.

Draping the skin over his shoulders, the donkey hid in the under-brush. Each animal that passed by took one look at the lion's tawny fur and heavy mane and fled for his life.

Then, through the trees, the donkey glimpsed the red flash of a fox's tail. Quickly he hid himself again. "That fox has called me a fool too often," the donkey thought. "We'll see who's the fool now!" As the fox came trotting along the path, the donkey jumped out of the bushes and let out a deafening "Hee-haw!"

The fox laughed. "You might have frightened me with that lion's skin," he said, "if you hadn't opened your mouth."

Fools can disguise themselves, but not their words.

THE CROW AND THE PITCHER

For weeks and weeks there had been no rain. The streams and pools had dried to dust, and all of the animals were thirsty. Two crows, flying together in search of water, spotted a pitcher that had been left on a garden wall. They flew to it and saw that it was half full of water. But neither one could reach far enough inside the pitcher's narrow neck to get a drink.

"There must be way to get that water," said the first crow. "If we think it through, we'll find an answer."

The second crow tried to push the pitcher over, straining with all of his might. But it was too heavy to budge. "It's hopeless!" he croaked, and flew away to look for water elsewhere.

But the first crow stayed by the pitcher and thought, and after a time he had an idea. Picking up some small pebbles in his beak, he dropped them one by one into the pitcher until at last the water rose to the brim. Then the clever bird happily quenched his thirst.

Wisdom and patience succeed where force fails.

THE CHILDREN AND THE FROGS

A group of children gathered near a pond and began to skip rocks across the water. They laughed and cheered as the rocks skimmed over the surface, sending plumes of spray flying.

Meanwhile, a family of frogs who lived in the pond cowered among the lily pads, terrified of the stones that flew and splashed all around them. At last one brave frog dared to poke her head out of the water.

"For pity's sake, please stop!" she begged. "It's only a game to you, but it's life and death to us!"

One person's play is another's grief.

THE TRAVELERS
AND THE GOLD COINS

Two traveling companions were walking along the road, when one of them spied a leather sack lying in the dirt. Picking it up, he discovered that it was heavy with gold coins.

"What luck!" he exclaimed. "I've found a treasure!"

"Don't you mean '*We've* found a treasure'?" asked his companion. "Didn't we agree to share *all* the fortunes of the road?"

"You're a fool if you think I'm going to share this," retorted the first traveler. "I'm the one who found it and it's mine to keep."

Just then, the two heard a mob of angry people up ahead. "Stop, thief! Bring back that gold!" they cried out, running toward the travelers, waving axes and stout staffs of wood.

"We're done for!" grieved the man who had found the purse. "They'll be sure to think we're thieves. They'll kill us both!"

"Oh, no!" said his companion. "You found the gold, not me. Remember, it's yours to keep!"

If you don't share your good luck, don't expect to share your bad.

THE BOASTING TRAVELER

A man who had traveled to distant lands returned to his hometown. He stood in the marketplace, boasting of his adventure: he had climbed the highest mountains, sailed the deepest seas, and visited the most magnificent cities.

"But the most amazing thing of all," he declared, "was when a foolish man there challenged me to a jumping contest, and I made the longest, most spectacular leap that was ever seen. Why, no one else in the world had ever jumped so far! You can ask anyone there and they'll tell you the same."

One of the crowd grew tired of the traveler's bragging. "There's no need to ask anyone at all," he called out. "Just make the same leap here, and we'll see with our own eyes how far you can jump!"

Deeds count more than words.

THE ANT AND THE DOVE

A dove in flight spied an ant struggling in the creek below, near to drowning. In pity, she lowered a blade of grass into the water so that the ant might cling to it. "Friend, you have saved my life," the ant said gratefully, as he was lead safely to shore.

Beside the creek stood a hunter, who raised his bow to take aim at the dove. Seeing his rescuer in danger, the tiny ant crawled up the hunter's boot and stung the hunter on the leg. With a cry of pain the hunter let his arrow fly off the mark, and the dove was free from danger.

One good turn deserves another.

THE DOG AND THE BONE

A dog carrying a bone looked over the edge of the bridge and saw his own reflection in the water below.

"Look at that dog," he thought. "Why, the bone he's carrying looks much bigger than mine. Juicier, too, and full of meat. If only I could have that bone as well! If I bark as loud as I can, maybe that will scare him into dropping his bone and running away."

But as he opened his mouth to bark, his own bone fell with a splash into the river, leaving the foolish dog with nothing at all.

Don't give up what's real for what isn't.

THE LION AND THE GNAT

"How dare you disturb my rest!" a lion growled at a gnat who buzzed too close to his twitching ear. "Be off, before I crush you into dust!"

"Brave words!" jeered the tiny gnat. "But I'm not afraid of you. For all your boasting, you'd never dare to meet me in battle!"

With a roar of rage, the lion lunged at the gnat. But the tiny insect slipped easily between his claws and flew to sting him on the nose. The lion swatted at him, but managed only to scratch and tear at his own face. Again and again the gnat bit the lion; again and again the lion drew his own blood, trying to capture his enemy. At last, exhausted and in pain, the lion bellowed, "Enough! I surrender!"

The least of our enemies can be the deadliest.

THE WOLF AND THE SHEPHERD

As a wolf lay hidden near a shepherd's home, he smelled a rich, mouth-watering fragrance in the air. Creeping close to the window, he saw the shepherd and his family feasting together on roasted mutton.

"If *I* catch and eat one of their sheep," the wolf grumbled, "they set the dogs on me. But here they are, doing the very same thing themselves!"

We often condemn others for what we see no wrong in doing ourselves.

THE OAK AND THE REEDS

A magnificent oak stood proudly by a quiet pool, and at its feet grew a cluster of modest, slender reeds. Whenever a great wind blew, the tree stood as strong as a mountain, reaching its limbs high to the sky. But the reeds would bend and bow low to even the gentlest breeze.

"No wind can ever make *me* bow my head," the proud oak boasted.

"Wait and see," whispered the reeds as they swayed with the wind. "Wait and see."

Soon there came a furious storm. The reeds were shaken and tossed in the gusts, first this way, then that. The mighty oak stood tall and straight, defying the storm. But the winds came faster and fiercer, and at last the oak's roots were torn from the ground. It fell with a terrible crash.

When the storm passed and the morning light came, the reeds stood tall again. "You see?" they said softly to the fallen oak. "We bowed to the wind and we survived; you resisted and perished."

It is better to bend than to break.

THE ROOSTER AND THE FOX

One evening at sunset a rooster flew up to his favorite perch in a tall pine tree. He had barely tucked his head beneath his wing when he heard something stirring below. He peered out and saw a fox sitting on the ground, panting excitedly.

"Hello, friend Rooster! Have you heard the news?" the fox called out.

"What news?" asked the rooster suspiciously.

"A truce has been declared!" replied the fox. "All the animals have chosen to live in peace. Even the lion and the wolf agreed! I came at once to tell you. Won't you come down, so we may embrace as true friends at last?"

But the rooster was too old and wise to trust a fox so easily. And he decided to put the fox's words to a test.

"Why, of course I'll come down," the rooster answered. "But tell me, friend Fox, did the dogs agree to this truce as well?"

"Of course, of course!" answered the fox, licking her lips.

"Then those two dogs that I can see from here," remarked the rooster, craning his neck, "must be coming to celebrate with us. This way! Over here!" he called loudly.

"Dogs? Oh, my!" stammered the fox. "I'm afraid I can't stay. My children are waiting for me at home. We must celebrate another time!" And the fox was off as fast as she could run.

Tricksters are easily tricked.

BELLING THE CAT

A large family of mice made their home behind the walls of a fine old house. It would have been a life of luxury except for one thing: a cat lived in the house, a sleek and stealthy hunter with gleaming eyes. Silent as a ghost on her padded feet, she would pounce, capturing one unlucky victim in her claws and sending the rest fleeing for safety.

At last the mice called a meeting to decide what should be done about their deadly enemy. They talked and argued for hours, until one young mouse raised his voice. "Why are you wasting all of this time?" he cried. "The answer is perfectly simple! We'll just tie a bell around the neck of the cat, and then we'll always hear her coming."

"Brilliant! A remarkable plan! Our troubles are over!" cried the mice. But then one wise old mouse, who had not spoken before, stepped forward.

"This is a very clever plan," he said, "except for one thing. My friends, which of us has the courage to tie the bell around the cat?"

Brave words are easier than brave deeds.

THE MERMAID AND THE WOODCUTTER

A woodcutter had been hard at work all day, cutting down trees to sell for firewood. It was nearing sunset, but he wanted to cut one last tree before going home for the night. Coming across a sturdy elm that grew beside a deep pool, he set to work. But he was so tired that, after a few strokes, his ax slipped out of his hands and fell with a splash into the deep black water.

"How could I be so careless!" the woodcutter cried. "I'll never see my ax again!" And he stood by the water in despair.

Now, a mermaid happened to be nearby, and heard the woodcutter's lamentations. Quick as thought, the creature appeared before him and asked him what was wrong.

"I've lost my only ax in the water," the woodcutter groaned. "I can't afford to buy another, and now my children will go hungry. What can I do?"

"Wait here," the mermaid replied, and she dived to the bottom of the pool. When she came back to the surface, she held in her hand an ax made of pure gold.

"Is this the ax you lost?" the mermaid asked the woodcutter.

"No, that one isn't mine," the honest man answered.

The mermaid dived again to the bottom of the pool, and came up with a shining silver ax. "Then this one must be yours," she said.

"No, that one's not mine, either," sighed the woodcutter. "Mine was just a plain iron ax with a wooden handle."

For a third time the mermaid dived to the bottom of the pool, and this time she came up with an old, worn iron ax.

"That's the one!" cried the woodcutter joyfully. "How can I ever thank you?"

"My friend," said the mermaid, "your honesty deserves a reward.

Take all three axes home with you, and your children will never go hungry again."

When the delighted woodcutter reached home, he told his family what had happened. Now, the woodcutter had a brother who, when he heard the story, said to himself, "Why should my foolish brother have better luck than me? Tomorrow I'll try the same trick, and I'll come home wealthy, too!"

The next day the woodcutter's brother went to the same pool, and promptly threw his ax into the water. Immediately he began weeping and wailing, calling on the mermaid to help him. The mermaid appeared and, diving to the bottom of the pool, brought up a golden ax. "Is this the one you lost?" she asked.

"That's the one!" the woodcutter's brother cried.

But the mermaid let the golden ax fall back beneath the water. "For your dishonesty," she said, "you'll have no ax at all." And then she vanished, leaving the woodcutter's brother poorer than ever.

Honesty is the best policy.

INDEX OF FABLES

"This is a very clever plan," the wise old mouse said, "except for one thing. My friends, which of us has the courage to tie the bell around the cat?"